Parker B. Davis

Tangled Rhymes

Parker B. Davis

Tangled Rhymes

ISBN/EAN: 9783337271961

Printed in Europe, USA, Canada, Australia, Japan

Cover: Foto ©Andreas Hilbeck / pixelio.de

More available books at **www.hansebooks.com**

Tangled Rhymes:

BY

PARKER B. DAVIS.

PORTLAND, ME.

FORD & RICH, PRINTERS AND PUBLISHERS.

1889.

INDEX.

Tangled Rhymes.

BONNY WOODS OF MAINE.

LET others sing of sunny lands,
　　Where sultry breezes blow
Through orange trees and olive groves,
　　And limped waters flow;
Of fair Italia's sunlit strand,
　　Or the vine-clad hills of Spain;
But dearer far than these to me
　　Are the bonny woods of Maine.

Though rough and tangled they may be,
　　And bound with ice and snow,
Yet hearts have here a quicker throb,
　　And cheeks a brighter glow;
And eyes put on a braver look
　　With health in every vein—
True freedom lives among us here
　　Within the woods of Maine.

From where Atlantic casts her foam
　Upon Old Orchard's strand,
To where Katahdin lifts her head
　Above our forest land,
Are hearts as true as earth has known,
　And hands without a stain
That point with joyous pride, today,
　To the grand old woods of Maine.

And tho gh the wealth of lands remote
　May please the eye the best,
Yet, oh! within the woods of Maine,
　'Tis here the heart can rest;
And though her sons may wander far,
　By mountain land or plain,
Their hearts turn back with longing still
　To the bonny woods of Maine.

MAINE TO CHARLESTON.

[1886.]

ON the south wind comes a murmur,
   To this piny land of ours,
Bringing us a tale of anguish
   From that sunny land of flowers:

Telling us that where old ocean
   Rolls her waters full and free,
Hearts are sad and homes are stricken,
   Down at Charleston by the sea.

Telling us that famed St. Michael's
   Cloud-bathed head is reeling now,
While the livid drops of terror
   Stand on many a dusky brow.

Years ago, when war's first cannon
   Blazed from out your open gate,
Then our hearts grew hard and bitter
   With the burning fires of hate:

How we longed for northern thunders
   All your sturdy walls to shake ;
How our guns were manned and mustered
   All your southern pride to break.

Now, when ruin falls upon you
   With this dire and awful blow,
All our hearts go out in weeping
   For your hearth-stones smitten low ;

And we reach a hand unto you.
   O'er the years which intervene,
O'er the graves of sleeping heroes,
   Blue and gray, which lie between ;

And from every crag and valley,
   Through this land so rough and free.
Prayers go up for God to help you—
   Down at Charleston by the sea.

BE IN EARNEST.

OF whatever land or nation,
High or lowly be your station,
And whatever your occupation,
Would you mend your situation,
    Be in earnest.

In the field or forest glen,
Or among the haunts of men,
With the sword or with the pen,
If you fail just try again :—
    Be in earnest.

Should the work of many years
Only bring you idle jeers,
You've no time for foolish tears ;
Labor on ere night appears :—
    Be in earnest.

Let each deed and thought be pure,
And each stepping stone be sure :
Though temptations may allure,
Build up work that shall endure :—
    Be in earnest.

Do your noblest day by day—
Honest work will surely pay :
Do not waste the time in play,
Do not dream your life away :—
　　　Be in earnest.

Dreams are not for waking hours—
Sterner duties need your powers,
Ere you wait in shady bowers,
With your feet among the flowers,
　　　Be in earnest.

Never doubt your strength to do :
If your aims are only true
This great world is needing you—
In the end you'll get your due :
　　　Be in earnest.

Step from out the idle herd
And your armor tightly gird :
Hearts of nations oft are stirred
By a well-timed deed or word :—
　　　Be in earnest.

✛ FATE. ✛

WE met to-day in the careless throng,
   Clasped hands in a formal way,
And never a word of ours betrayed
   Thoughts of another day:

But a glance of the blue eyes spoke to me
   What others could not know,
And I felt your heart go back with mine
   To a day in the long ago.

A picture rose from out the past
   I know you saw it too,
That memory swept away the years
   hat hid the scene from view :—

A woodland path 'mong maples tall,
   A boy and girl together,
A gleam of blue sky up above,
   The glorious summer weather :

The blue eyes glancing into his,
　The blushing face so fair,
The sunlight, checkered by the leaves
　'Mong waves of dark brown hair ;

The sweet old story told anew,
　While hearts creep close together,
And birds above repeat the vows
　Of love and trust forever.

To you, I know that other lips,
　Have told the tale since then ;
And as for me—well, I've been out
　In the ranks of busy men :

And I had thought this past was dead,
　And buried 'mong the years ;
That never more your eyes had power
　To waken hopes or fears :

I've seen today how vain the thought.
　How weak man's strength appears,
When just a glance from eyes of blue
　Undoes the work of years.

Today we stand by the cruel gulf
   That fate has fixed between,
While a breath of that far-off summer brings
   Mad thoughts of what, "might have been."

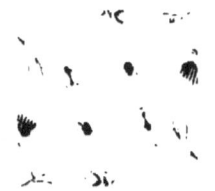

UP OR DOWN.

RIEND, you say you're only waiting
    Some more favored time or place;
That you're counting all your chances,
    And you mean to win the race;

But you never stop to reckon
    That you're on a moving stream,
With the current flowing downward,
    Where the danger lights are seen;

That you cannot stop or linger,
    Though the tempests o'er you frown—
On the stream of life, my brother,
    You are going up or down.

If you wait for friendly breezes,
    While you idly lie and dream,
Oh! so sad will be your waking—
    For you're floating down the stream.

When those friendly breezes greet you
   It may be too late for you ;
For the current's growing stronger,
   And the breakers come in view.

Now's the time to turn and struggle.
   Would you win a victor's crown,
You must pull against the current—
   When you drift you're going down.

Sunny skies and pleasant waters
   Wait to greet you up ahead,
While the clouds are dark below you,
   And the lightning flashes red :

Up above sweet flowers are blooming ;
   Down below lost wretches drown—
On the stream of life, my brother,
   You are going up or down.

YEAR BY YEAR.

YEAR by year the World goes round,
　　As it has for countless ages,
Spite of learning most profound,
　　And the wisdom of the sages.

Year by year, with ceaseless motion,
　　Though its friction ought to stop it;
'Way up here in space suspended—
　　Not a rainbow, e'en, to prop it.

Year by year it gives us sunshine,
　　Year by year some cloudy weather;
And, by logic, one must follow,
　　Since they cannot come together.

So, who cares if skies are heavy?
　　They will brighten, never fear:
Clouds are only prophets, telling
　　That a better time is near.

Laws of change are fixed by nature,
  Though we know not how it's done :
No life always runs in shadow,
  Neither always in the sun.

Griefs are only what we're paying
  For the joys that next appear :
Aching hearts will soon be happy :
  Smiles will chase away the tear.

Take the sweets and question never ;
  No use grumbling at the price,
Or you'll find they're passing from you—
  They are seldom offered twice :

And tomorrow's pressing onward
  In the footsteps of to-day,
And to-day will soon be fleeting,
  Nevermore to cross our way.

We are living in the present,
  And can ne'er recall the past :
No use grieving over follies—
  Only let their lessons last.

Year by year we see more clearly
　　There are things we may not know;
There are depths we may not fathom,
　　Heights to which we may not go.

Vain it is to measure problems
　　Which we cannot solve below;
Better far to sip the pleasures
　　As they swiftly come and go.

Just to take things as we find them;
　　Make the most of what they are;
Problems grasp that we can handle;
　　Never soar above too far;

Keep in mind this earth was moving
　　Long before our natal morn,
And will still go whirling onward
　　Just the same when we are gone;

That the world we cannot manage,
　　Though it may seem out of gear,—
These are lessons we are learning
　　One by one and year by year.

HAVE AN OBJECT.

THERE'S a rare old eastern fable—
  The wisdom of which you'll find—
By some turn of fortune's table
  Brought oft before my mind :

A frightened hare—runs the story—
  Pursued by a greyhound fleet,
'Neath trees so old and hoary
  Pressed on with flying feet,

Till pursuit was given over,
  And the greyhound paused for breath,
While the hare 'neath friendly cover
  Sped on from a cruel death.

A woodsman rallied the laggard
  Who failed in the wild-wood chase,
As naught but a worthless braggart,
  Since the hare had won the race ;

But the loser answered his mocking
  With these words of wisdom fine
(For hounds are prone to talking
  In that far off eastern clime :)

" You should not judge our powers
  By this race through the tangled green ;
If an equal prize were ours,
  A difference you'd have seen :

" For I ran just for a dinner,
  It was all I had in view ;
While he, should he prove the winner,
  Would ransom his life he knew."

Now the moral is clear, my reader,
  As clear as the deep blue sky :
In the race you may be a leader
  If you place your standard high.

The object for which you're living,
  More than your native fleetness,
Will honest power be giving,
  And lead to life's completeness.

LOVE AMONG THE ANGELS.

WHAT is love among the Angels?
   Tell me true how Angels love,
You who paint to us poor sinners
   All the garnered joys above.

For we have a way of loving,
   Though it's crude and old we know,
Yet since Adam ate the apple,
   It has served us here below.

And, with reverence, let me say
   That I like this simple bliss,
And I wouldn't give a nickel
   For a better love than this.

So you tell, and tell me truly,
   For I really want to hear,
How do angels tell the story
   'That we mortals find so dear?

Do they press the lips as warmly?
  Is the hand-clasp just as tight?
Is the kiss as sweetly thrilling?
  Are those angel eyes so bright?

Can they feel the bosom's heaving,
  While the heart beats wild and free?
Is this love among the angels?
  Praying saint, come answer me.

If it isn't, then I tell you,
  Yes, I tell you fair and true,
If I reach that golden portal
  And am bid to enter through,

It will be when evening shadows
  Make the heavenly gateway dim;
And I know a little angel
  That I'll try to smuggle in—

Just a little human angel,
  Without wings or plumage rare,
But with all her mortal garments,
  And a rosebud in her hair.

And when we have passed St. Peter,
  And have gained the golden street,
By the groups of singing angels
  We shall haste with eager feet,

Till we gain some quiet corner,
  Where the stars forget to shine ;
Then while hearts beat on together,
  With her dainty hand in mine,

We will listen to the music,
  To its swelling soft and low,
But we'll never raise our voices—
  For they'd find us then, you know.

SUNNY PLACES.

—⟩⟨—

WHEN a shadow falls around us,
  And all lovely light effaces,
We should never be discouraged,
  Life has many sunny places.

Oh! such bright and sunny places,
  Scattered all along life's highway,
Where the light of love streams on us
  From each widely open by-way.

We should never count the shadows
  Which our own cold hearts have brought us,
But with grateful hearts, and happy,
  Mind the lesson life has taught us—

That we may grope on in darkness,
  Slowly on, with somber faces,
Or, by hastening through the shadows,
  Linger long in sunny places.

A HEART SONG.

THEY say there's a purer, better life,
　　Than the one we're living here,
With never a taint of sin or strife,
　　And never a cause of fear ;—
But, oh ! my heart will fondly cling
　　To the joys of life below ;
And not for life where the angels sing,
　　Would I change the joys I know.

We're told there's a home of eternal joy
　　In that spirit land above,
Where the hopes we cherish have no alloy,
　　In that home of boundless love ;—
But, oh ! my heart will fondly cling
　　To the joys of life below ;
And not for life where the angels sing,
　　Would I change the joys I know.

For I see not clearly beyond the grave—
   I know there are pleasures here—
And I'd rather a world of troubles brave
   Than enter the solemn bier:
For, oh! my heart will fondly cling
   To the joys of life below;
And not for life where the angels sing,
   Would I change the joys I know.

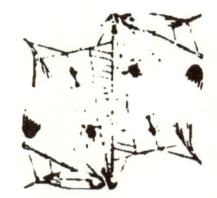

UNCLE SAM'S BIRTHDAY.

"WHAT means this stir in Rome" today?
　　This dread and dire commotion?
This surging tumult, spreading out
　　From ocean unto ocean?

The boom of cannon, roll of drum,
　　The small boy's dreadful clatter?
What horrid fate's upon us now—
　　O, tell me what's the matter?

Does foreign foe invade our land
　　In search of blood and plunder,
To hunt us down with sword and brand,
　　And scare us with his thunder?

Or have those Redskins gone again
　　From starving reservations,
With blood and fire and tomahawks,
　　To hunt for scalps and rations?

Or has a Babel broken loose
   Within our quiet border,
To stir up all this din and strife,
   Against all law and order?

"Tut! tut! my son, there's nothing wrong,
   No dreaded foe's approaching,
No Redskin band with bloody hand
   Upon our homes encroaching:

'Tis only Uncle's birthday, lad,
   That's why we make a noise;
For Uncle Sam is youthful yet,
   And so we all are boys.

'Tis little more than a hundred years
   Since the hero came to life,
So you see he's only a stripling yet
   In all this din and strife.

He's lusty, though, and growing fast,
   And strong beyond his years;
He's heard the sound of guns before—
   No smoke and noise he fears.

At Yorktown once he took the sword
  Of George the Third, you know,
Who owned the youngster struggled well,
  And struck a weighty blow.

At Chippewa and Lundy's Lane
  He proved his mettle good ;
And down by the Crescent City, there,
  Among the cotton stood.

And when those sun-tanned Mexic boys
  Were wanting northern land,
He clutched his trusty sword again
  And crossed the Rio Grande ;

And Santa Anna thought the price
  Of northern lands was high ;
And though he liked the property
  He couldn't afford to buy.

He had his family quarrel once
  As other people do :
Concerning this, I only say,
  He brought his standard through.

And now he stands in peace today,
   With laurels on his brow,
The strongest youth the world can boast—
   To whom the nations bow :

And so, you see, 'tis proper, quite,
   We celebrate today,
With music such as heroes know,
   Who win the deathless bay.

⇥DOES IT?⇤

WHERE the land and waters meet,
We two roamed in converse sweet,
Conning love's sweet lesson o'er—
All its soft delicious lore—
Learning of it more and more,
On a summer day of yore.

Now we roam no more together
In the bright and sunny weather,
For my feet have gone astray
Since that sunny, summer day,
When we wandered down the way
Where the broken sea-weeds lay.

And I wonder does your heart
Into quicker beating start,
When your cheek is softly fanned
By the breezes o'er the sand,
Where we wandered hand in hand—
Where the waters meet the land?

RETROSPECTION.

LOOKING back along the pathway
    Which we've traveled through the years;
Noting all the woes and heart-aches,
    All the bitter pains and tears ;

Living o'er those boyish fancies,
    All those dreams of fame again,
Saddened now by one low murmur,
    Softly sighing " might have been."

For those dreams and aspiration,
    Hopes and longings deep and true,
Were as chaff before the whirlwind,
    When life's stormy tempests blew ;

And their wrecks are lying scattered
    All along life's backward way—
Stranded hopes and broken idols,
    Which we cherished day by day.

Yet we feel that from these losses
  Better hopes were born to live ;
Purer dreams and aspirations,
  More refined than youth can give ;

And from out those shattered ruins
  Flowers of promise bud and blow,
And our hearts are purer, better,
  For the sorrows that we know :

For they teach us many lessons—
  Lessons conned through bitter tears—
That shall keep us from the shallows,
  And the reefs, in coming years.

So we feel that on life's voyage
  Much that's truly good and grand
May be traced to broken idols,
  Lying shattered on the strand.

WATCHING THE SHIPS.

OH! Lady fair,
  With sunny hair,
Go back no thoughts to-day
    To a far off time
    In a golden clime,
In the beauteous month of May?

    When side by side,
    By the heaving tide,
Where scented breezes play,
    With silent lips,
    We watched the ships
Go sailing down the bay?

    For lips are dumb
    When sweet thoughts come—
And sweet were ours that day,
    On the shining strand,
    In that summer land,
In the beauteous month of May.

But love can speak
From blushing cheek,
And eyes of heavenly blue ;
And blosom's swell
The tale would tell,
Though lips no language knew.

O ! had I told
The story old,
Fair lady, then, to you,
No ocean wide,
With restless tide,
Would roll between us two.

But were it so,
I do not know
If it were well, or ill ;
I can but feel
Sweet longings steal
Through all my being still.

And years I'd give
Could I but live
Once more that happy day,
On the golden strand,
In that sunny land,
In the beauteous month of May.

BEECHER.

ONCE more the bells on a nation's ear,
　　With mournful cadence swelling,
Of a people's loss and a victor's gain
　　Their solemn tale are telling.

They tell a tale of hearts that bleed,
　　Of hopes that are buried low,
Of anguish deep for the loved one gone
　　Which only the stricken know.

They speak to us of a life work done—
　　A work that was all complete,
Wrought out in love for the good of man,
　　And laid at the Master's feet—

A work that shall reach through ages vast,
　　Growing ever more bright and grand,
With its holy luster spreading out
　　To the gates of the promised land.

And all the laurels that mortal hands
  Can weave for that gifted brow,
And all the tributes a people bring,
  They are vain and worthless now;

But with trembling hand we twine this **wreath**
  For the grave of the hero dead,
And drop it down with a nation's tears
  On that hero's lonely bed.

CASTLES IN THE AIR.

THROUGH this busy life of ours,
'Mong its thorns or springing flowers,
Oh, such joy, ecstatic, rare,
Building "Castles in the air!"

From the lazy tramping drone,
To the monarch on his throne,
Rich and poor, and high and low,
O'er this world where'er we go,

All are looking on ahead,
By their fancies fondly led,
On through dreamy realms so fair,
Up to "Castles in the air."

One sees food and clothing vast,
And his tramping all is past;
And the other, kingdoms won
In all lands beneath the sun.

And we look beyond the gloom
Of the damp and chilly tomb,
To a home without a care,
Bright, eternal, in the air.

From the redman, homeward bound
To his happy hunting-ground,
Through Mahomet's wandering school,
Where the Koran gives the rule,

Up to favored Brooklyn Height,
Where a Beecher sheds the light,
Leading on through pastures rare,
Up to " Castles in the air."

All expect to find above
What their hearts have learned to love.
Well, I hope, beyond the river
Shutting out this life forever,

That our castles may be stronger,
And may give us shelter longer,
Than the ones we're watching here
Falling round us year by year.

And I've often noticed this :
That we many troubles miss,
And our lives are fashioned fair,
By our " Castles in the air."

So we'll build our castles high,
Build them to the blue domed sky
Build our castles though they fall—
Better so than none at all.

Though our lives be bright or sad,
Checkered o'er with good or bad,
Oh, 'tis bliss beyond compare,
Building " Castles in the air !"

QUESTIONINGS.

———→‹←———

WHEN this fair, brief life is o'er,
When this body lives no more,
When I pass death's gloomy shore—
   What then?

When those clustered round my bed,
Through their tears have sadly said—
Murmured softly—"he is dead"—
   What then?

Is this death the way we rise
To a home beyond the skies,
Where the blest one never dies—
   Is it?

Is this life but to prepare
For a beauteous mansion there,
Filled with all the heart calls fair—
   Is it?

Shall we gather those we love
In that Eden-land above,
And in joy forever rove—
    Shall we?

Shall we press the lips in Heaven
Which on earth to ours are given,
When these bonds of life are riven—
    Shall we?

Can I solve the mystery out?
Can I pierce the veil of doubt
Which enwraps these thoughts about—
    Can I?

Can I find some one below
Who to me the way will show,
How the doubting heart may *know*—
    Can I?

ONLY THREE.

I sit alone in my room tonight
   With a pictured group before me,
And thoughts of a happy springtime gone
   Come slowly stealing o'er me.

Five happy faces look in mine,
   With bright eyes full of glee;
But, oh! how sadly comes the thought,
   Tonight we're only three.

I think how bright the world spread out
   In that glorious May-time weather,
As we stood with eager, waiting feet
   Upon life's verge together.

What dreams of coming joys were ours,
   What hopes and plans we cherished
That since along life's rugged way
   In silent gloom have perished;

For one soon found the thorny way
   Too rough for further going,
And o'er her silent form tonight
   The winter winds are blowing.

And now that other, who so long
   Has lingered by the river,
With eyes that bravely faced the gloom
   Has closed those eyes forever.

And, oh! how hard to reconcile
   Dreams of that sunny May,
With thoughts of that worn and wasted form
   That lies so still to-day.

Five years, my classmates, hardly brings
   What youthful fancy painted ;
Oh! could we then have raised the veil
   Our hearts had surely fainted.

As I put away that pictured group
   This thought comes over me ;
Are we still five as on that May,
   Or are we—only three ?

THE SAME OLD STORY.

THE same old story told last night
  In accents low and sweet,
While the smiling moon flung down her light
  Around your happy feet.

Yes, just the story, short and old,
  But, oh! so very dear,
That's told in every land and clime
  When rosy lips are near—

The self-same story told of yore,
  In whispers soft and low,
Beneath a palm-trees spreading shade,
  In Eden, long ago;

The same old story that was told
  To Grecian Hellen fair;
And Highland Mary heard that tale
  On banks of bonny Ayr.

And while this world goes round and **round**
  To give us light and shade,
And waters flow and grasses grow,
  And flowers bloom and fade,

That tale will e'er be told anew,
  And ever seem as dear,
When hearts are light and eyes are **bright**
  And rosy lips are near.

ONLY LIFE.

ONLY a dream of the morrow,
　　To strengthen the heart to-day;
Only a hope of the future,
　　To lighten the weary way:

Only a ray of the sunshine
　　We're longing to call our own;
Only a few stray flowerets
　　Along the pathway strown:

Only a sip of the nectar
　　Would fill our lives with bliss;
Only a gleam of a better,
　　A purer way than this:

Only a sweet, eager longing,
　　For heights that we cannot reach;
Only a sad treasured lesson,
　　Which naught but the past can teach:

Only some sacred memories,
　　Kept green by our falling tears,
Wafted back to our hearts again
　　From the dead and buried years:

Only a light in the valley,
　　Revealing a home above;
Only a golden gateway,
　　That opes to the key of love.

BY THE RIO GRANDE.

I stood where the Rockies' gloomy heights
   Frown down on that sterile land
That stretches away in a barren waste
   Along by the Rio Grande.

Above me the snow-clad mountain peaks
   Lined clear on the western sky:
Below me, the dreamy Mexic town
   And the river rolling by:

Around me, the sage and cotton wood
   And stunted cactus growing:
And o'er it all the mountain breeze
   With cooling freshness blowing.

I'd wandered where some clustered graves,
   Heaped up in the drifting sand,
Told some had paused in the race for gold
   In that rugged mountain land;

And I read on slabs erected there
　By awkward but friendly hands,
The names of those who had given all
　For rest in those lonely sands.

At length I paused by the side of one,
　Whose inscription, rude and deep,
Told a tale to me of him who lay
　In his final awful sleep.

" Russell Murry, aged twenty-four ;
　Was shot by an unknown hand :"
This the inscription that I read that day
　By the rolling Rio Grande.

I read far more than these brief words ;
　For a picture rose to view,
I saw the spires of a distant town
　Which the sleeping miner knew.

Down at the foot of a grassy hill
　Where the evening shadows play,
I saw a farm-house nestling there
　With its roof-tree old and gray;

I saw once more the parting scene,
　A mother's sobs and tears—
The aching hearts that are aching still
　Through all these weary years.

Then the days of anxious waiting,
  Till the first glad letter came ;
Oh ! such words of tender greeting,
  Written o'er that well-loved name.

Then the dreary months that followed,
  Sometimes bringing news of him,
Often only pain and longing,
  When those watching eyes grew dim.

Then the awful void, the waiting
  For the word that never came ;
Then a formal note of horror.
  Written o'er a stranger's name.

Oh ! the breaking hearts that read it,
  And the hopes that died that day—
Buried deep with the loved one, lying
  In that grave so far away.

As all this tale rose up to view,
  What wonder with tender hand
I straightened the slab of that lonely grave
  By the rolling Rio Grande.

SHERIDAN.

SOLDIER, rest! the battle's done:
Peace be thine; the victory's won.
Though a nation now may weep thee,
It were wrong for us to keep thee;
For beyond death's mystic vale,
Thou hast heard the well known hail;
Felt the welcome, warm and true,
Of thy gallant boys in blue;—
Clasped the hands of those who died
Fighting bravely by thy side,
When, amidst war's shot and shell,
Freedom's banner rose and fell,
And we know the rapturous thrill
All thy soldier heart must fill.
As they close their ranks around
The hero-leader they have found.

Laurel wreath we twine to-day
For our soldier passed away,
And our humble tributes bring
Unto thee, our battle king.
Dearer still thy name will grow
As the years shall come and go;
And when ages long have rolled,
This people shall thy memory hold—
Millions now unborn shall thrill
At the name of "Little Phil."

A MEMORY.

ONLY a memory, tender and sweet,
    Set to the music, soft and low,
Which the whispering breezes bear
    From the vale of the long ago.

And yet my heart-chords thrill again,
    With all the olden pleasure,
As memory shows this hidden page
    Among her hoarded treasure.

Ay, guard it well, that golden spot
    Upon time's rolling river;
For, oh! the joy it brought to me
    Has left my heart forever.

CONTEST ENDED.

THE race is run, the work is done;
   I stand in the gloaming now,
While the cooling breeze from the drooping **trees**
   Sweeps o'er my heated brow.

The race is run, the prizes won,
   But they fell to other hands:
From the course I go, with no gains to show
   For the race o'er the heated sands—

No garlands gay, no drooping bay,
   No sign of the world's renown;
I tried in the race for a forward place,
   But a part of the time I was down.

Though sorely beat by lighter feet,
   And oft from the pathway cast,
I held my way through the heated day,
   Nor tripped those running past.

So with conscience clear, I'm standing here,
  Where the cooling south wind blows :
I did my best, among the rest,
  And struggled in at the close.

Though no Triumph gay, in the olden way,
  Shall ever sound my praise,
Nor marble rise to the vaulted skies,
  To tell where my frame decays,

Yet I know that some, when the final drum
  Shall summon us all to meet,
Will render thanks for the clownish pranks
  That made me so easy beat.

MEMORIAL.

WE gather once more with tributes of flowers
  To wreathe o'er the graves of these heroes of
    ours,

With hearts that are thankful for all that they won;
For a country the grandest that's under the sun—

From Canada's snows to the Mexican wave
The sun never looks on a cowering slave;

But eyes are misty with sorrowful tears
As thoughts travel back o'er the swift rolling years,

And memory brings sad scenes to our view,
When were mustered together the brave and true.

Those parting scenes! how they rise before us,
Brought back by the thoughts that come surging
    o'er us—

The closely clasped hand and the tear-wet cheek,
The anguish too deep for the lips to speak,

The long-drawn kiss and the last embrace,
The lingering look at the well loved face :

Then some went marching away in the blue,
And some stood waiting with hearts as true—

Yes, waiting and trusting through the years,
Though hearts were breaking with anguish and fears.

And those who were waiting, perhaps, suffered more
Than they who the heat of the conflict bore ;

For brave hearts fighting, where the sun stands high
In the clear azure depth of that southern sky,

In the field of action found relief ;
In every victory they drowned their grief ;

For they felt that it shortened their time to roam—
That it brought them a little nearer to home.

Those battle scenes ! how they backward come,
With the stirring fife and beat of the drum ;

What scenes of anguish, of suffering and woe,
'Neath the scorching sun in that long ago—

The clasp of hands in the din and strife,
The last fond message for waiting wife,

The glazing eye of a comrade true,
The warm blood dyeing the Union blue,

The brave eyes turning to Freedom's flag,
With a glance of scorn for the Rebel rag;

And then those graves which we dug at dawn,
Where lie the fruits of the battle storm—

Where many a brave lies low to-day
In those unmarked graves so far away.

And as we gather with flowers and tears,
To garland the dead of those sad years,

We try to think what might have been lost;
But hearts turn back to the awful cost—

For hearts are stubborn things to guide,
Where love and duty are sundered wide.

We know we've a noble land today,
From the surf of Maine to 'Frisco bay;

From where Niagara's waters leap,
To the far-off shores of the Mexic deep;

We know that every soul is free,
However dark his skin may be;

We're thankful, too—or we try to be—
For the gift that made a nation free;

But our tears will drown the thanks we'd say,
For we only think of our dead to-day.

We think of a form in gallant blue,
And treasure the glance of eyes we knew;

And almost feel, though we know it's wrong—
But ties of love they bind so strong—

We almost feel that we'd give the gain
To look in those well-known eyes again,

And feel the clasp of a hand once more,
As firm and true as in days of yore.

We scatter flowers; 'tis all we can give,
To show they still in our memory live.

Flowers and tears for those who rest
'Neath the skies they loved the best;

Tears and flowers for those who lie
'Neath that far-off southern sky.

THE WANDERER'S TALE.

THANK you, sir, for your kindness,
  For food and shelter here;
But most of all, for sympathy,
  For friendly words and cheer.

For your food can only lengthen
  A life of bitter woe,
But pity and kindness bring me
  Bright pictures of long ago.

'Tis a lonely life, this tramping—
  An awful life I've led;
If I could but rest me sometimes,
  But O, this pain in my head

It urges me on forever,
  Through all the weary years.
I'm somewhat discouraged, to-day, sir,
  You'll excuse these foolish tears—

Perhaps they will make me better,
　And ease this dreary pain,
That has, for these twenty years,
　Been eating my heart and brain.

Perhaps this glimpse of home-life,
　With its quiet, peace, and rest,
Will stifle the bitter anger,
　That's raging within my breast.

I'm getting old and feeble,
　This tramping will soon be o'er;
How wrong my craving for vengeance,
　I never felt before.

I haven't the strength I had
　In the spring of sixty-one,
When I donned my country's blue,
　And marched 'neath a southern sun.'

My story? yes, I will tell it.
　A dreary one to hear,
But you'll learn why I talk so strange,
　And why my head is queer.

I'll draw you a picture of home—
　My home in the long ago,
Ere this pain came into my head,
　Or feet had wandered so.

In a green and sloping valley,
　Where Saco's waters glide,
Fringed round with shady woodlands,
　Where squirrels leap and hide,

Stands a dainty vine-wreathed cot ;
　Tall elms droop above it,
Flowers and birds make paradise—
　Nature seems to love it.

In the door-way stands a vision,
　Such as poet eyes may view
In the land of dream and fancy ;
　Such as earth gives but a few—

Lithesome figure, falling ringlets,
　O'er a brow of chastened white ;
Eyes as blue as heaven's ether ;
　O, so soft, and warm, and bright !

White robe falling, soft and fleecy,
　From her dainty, winsome height,
Makes her seem far less a woman
　Than an angel of the light.

God ! I've learned, by years of **anguish,**
　She was nothing but a woman :
All her fragile beauty hiding
　Heart so very, very human.

But I loved her with a passion
  Such as few can understand,
From the first sweet moment's clasping
  Of her dainty girlish hand.

And when at the altar standing
  I could claim that hand as mine,
All my life seemed turned to sunshine,
  And my blood seemed turned to wine.

'Twas such ecstatic joy to live —
  Just to live alone for her,
In that little vine-wreathed cot
  Where the flowers and sunshine were.

Then upon the tainted south-wind came
  The boom of a Rebel gun,
Whose shot was aimed at a nation's life—
  Of that nation I was one.

I am proud to-day, though it cost me all—
  But left me a heart to bleed—
That I answered at once my country's call
  In her hour of greatest need.

The smoke of Beauregard's cannon
  Still hung over Sumter's wall,
When under our starry banner
  I answered my country's call.

A clasping of hands at the dawning,
  The press of a tear-wet cheek,
The kiss that went with me to battle—
  Of these it is useless to speak.

And I need not recount the struggle,
  Its varied scenes you know;
I tried to do my duty ever,
  And kept my face to the foe.

Two years of fighting passed,
  Her letters, though so rare,
Were better to strengthen me
  Than all my southern fare:

And often I pressed to my lips
  A ringlet of golden hair,
And upward her name was wafted
  On the wings of a soldier's prayer.

When the letters ceased I wondered,
  But never a doubt crept in:
I watched and waited and saddened—
  But she was free from sin.

I'd sooner have doubted Heaven—
  Indeed, I believe I did:
For I thought that the hand of Fate
  Was keeping her letters hid.

And so I never forgot to write,
  I still believed her true,
The soldier's prayer was still the same,
  That ringlet 'neath the blue.

A year of agony passed—
  A year of torture—and then
I changed my active life
  For a Rebel prison pen.

I cannot picture to you
  My life in that filthy den ;
'Tis a blot on the human race
  That our captors there were men.

But I lived through those awful days,
  Kept hold on reason and life,
Never lost faith in my fellowman,
  Nor trust in that absent wife.

And at last an exchange was made ;
  I drank in God's pure air :
Never before, it seemed to me,
  Had the earth looked half so fair.

And yet I was only a wreck, at best,
  So worn and sick, but free ;
Yes, free to seek my home again—
  No more of battle for me.

O, how my heart went leaping forth,
  At the thought of home once more!
How I pictured o'er and o'er again
  My wife at the cottage door;—

The blue eyes, filled with tears for me,
  Look out o'er the valley way,
With trustful hope that never fails,
  Though pained by the long delay;

And then at my coming the eager start,
  That speaks her glad surprise;
The heaving bosom, trembling lips,
  The love in her tender eyes.

It seemed to me that all the time
  Of the years I'd been away,
Was yet as naught to the dreary time
  That now to our meeting lay.

But time rolls on though hearts may break,
  So the journey had an end—
My mind will fail me when I try
  To remember all, my friend.

I know I stole up the shaded walk
  To a closed forsaken door,
From which the light of home had fled,
  And would never greet me more.

I learned my wife had fled away
  With one I had known from youth :
On whom I would have staked my life.
  Without a doubt of his truth.

For many weeks I knew no more,
  But tossed on a fever-bed ;
Then struggled back to life once more,
  With this awful pain in my head.

And then I wandered away from there—
  That vale by the Saco's side.
I've sought for them through all the years.
  In my ramblings far and wide,

And I've always hoped to meet him,
  Stand face to face sometime,
And deal out a retribution
  In proportion to his crime.

I've forgiven her ; but as for him—
  They tell me there's one above
Who notes the smallest sparrow's fall.
  And holds us all in love.

I can't understand—its my head,
  It feels so dizzy and dim—
Why this punishment falls on me,
  Instead of falling on him.

I suppose we shall stand sometime
  At a great white throne afar,
And each receive a sentence fair
  At that dread tribunal bar :

But it seems to me now, sometimes,
  My poor head wanders so,
The reward to sin is better far
  Than to virtue, here below :

And I don't think I want that Heaven,
  Though its beauties shine so rare,
Unless in the happy gloaming
  I can clasp her hand up there—

Her hand with the stain washed from it,
  As pure, and fair, and white,
As the hand I held so proudly
  On that far-off bridal night.

For I know I should wander there,
  As I have in this sad life,
With this awful pain in my head,
  For a lost and sinful wife.

I thank you again for your kindness :
  This pain seems to urge me on :
I'm somewhat rested and strengthened,
  And so I'll have to be gone.

THE BROOKLET'S SONG

TO THE

LITTLE GIRL.

JUST listen now while I repeat
The song the brooklet sang so sweet.
Indeed it did, you needn't smile,
Brooklets sing just once in a while—
Not music only, I mean rhymes—
They sing real songs to me sometimes.

And brooklets have queer stories too :
Did they never tell their tale to you?
I doubt you know their language then,
It is'nt like the speech of men :
First it will murmur, low and sweet,
Creeping along beside my feet;

Then it will shout in merry glee,
Frolicking o'er a sunken tree ;
It has a tripping, joyous sound,
Leaping along the stony ground :
These sounds combine in some odd way
To form the song I heard that day.

They don't make words like ours, you know
With their vowel sounds that puzzle so,
I can't tell how the thought's expressed :
Perhaps the meaning's only guessed.
The music comes, you've heard that, sure,
It sounds so ringing bright and pure :

Into my soul there seems to creep
A language I try in vain to keep :
It leaves a tale remembered well,
Though how 'twas told 'tis hard to tell.
Sometimes the music brings no song
Though I may listen all day long,

But almost always when I go
Where those green willows droop so low,
And lie down there on the velvet grass
Close where the waters have to pass,
And close my eyes and listen long,
The dancing brooklet sings a song.

Asleep! why you're a real mean thing,
If I was I couldn't hear it sing.
Just listen now, I'll prove you're wrong,
For I remember all that song.
This was the brooklet's song that day,
I heard it plain from where I lay;
Not the words, but the meaning came,
I understood it just the same :—

" I wind about, and in and out,
　With here a blossom sailing,
And here and there a lusty trout,
　And here and there a grayling,

" And here and there a foamy flake
　Upon me as I travel,
And many a silvery waterbrake
　Above the golden gravel,

" And draw them all along, and flow
　To join the brimming river,
For men may come and men may go
　But I go on forever."

Heard it before? well, what of it?
I think 'twas sung because I love it.
I didn't say it *made* the song,
I wouldn't say that, because it's wrong :
Now you're laughing, well, I don't care,
Though I don't think it's really fair,
For the brooklet sang it, every word—
Or else I never could have heard.